CW00839872

by the same author
for children

How the Whale Became
Meet My Folks!
The Earth-Owl and Other Moon People
Nessie, the Mannerless Monster
The Coming of the Kings
The Iron Man
Moon-Whales
Season Songs
Under the North Star
What is the Truth?
Ffangs the Vampire Bat and the Kiss of Truth
Tales of the Early World
The Iron Woman
The Dreamfighter and Other Creation Tales
Collected Animal Poems volumes 1 to 4

SHAGGY
and
SPOTTY

TED HUGHES

with illustrations by David Lucas

For Frieda and Nicholas

The strong man, the hairy woman, the axe-thrower, the pie-eater, the mermaid in the glass tank, the fortune-teller, the talking horse,

The two dogs set off to the fair, for the music, the jollity, the shouts. They hear it in the distance. They go, faster, faster.

They arrive.

the strength testers, the coconut shies, the shooting galleries.

And what do they hear? The booming voice: 'Roll up, roll up!', and the music, the music, the music. But …

And what do they see?

What they really want is a ride on the roundabout. They climb on and they're away. Faster, faster. Shaggy wants to stop it, but how? Faster, faster. Spotty wants to get off. Faster, faster. And faster and faster till whoosh, WHOOSH. The two dogs are flung out over the heads of the crowd but no O not onto the ground O no!

They land in a dodgem car. The dodgem cars are whizzing and swivelling this way and that, everybody trying to bash into everybody else. Shaggy whirls the steering wheel one way, Spotty pulls it another way. O the screams, the wild faces, the sparks! Shaggy tries to drive right out of the hullaballoo and CRASH – the two dogs are shot out of their seats. They fly through the air but no O not onto the ground O no!

They land on the giant wheel. Up up up up. The world goes tiny far below. Then down down down down and the world rushes towards them. Then up up up up up. Then down down to crash them to the middle of the earth, then up, up, up and up and up and up and up – 'Jump!' cries Shaggy, and they jump.

And through the air the two dogs fall, down down they fall but no O not onto the ground O no!

They land in a car on the Wall of Death. Zoom,
zoom, round round round, the white faces, the
noise, the screams. Then hanging upside down,
the world tossed like a pancake.

Shaggy grabs the wheel and they zoom off into
space, turning over and over, and falling down
down but no O not onto the ground O no!

Perlonk! – They fall out of the car
and land on the switchback.
And whoosh they're away with
screaming people up and up and
down down and all the girls shriek,
all the boys go white, and up up up
and WHOOO.

Over the top then down steeper as
the girls shriek and the boys grip
their seats and grrrrrr up up up up
and WHOOO higher than ever,
nearly off into space but down down
down with the screams the white
stares and up up up up up up.

Ooooh – Shaggy grabs Spotty and
they jump. They jump into the air
and fall down down down but no
O not onto the ground O no no!

They land on the trampoline. Four strong men are holding the corners and they jerk. Up go the two dogs up and up. They see clouds and blue sky, they see tiny faces turned upwards, they see the tops of the marquees, as they turn over, over and down and down down and down and down but no O not onto the ground O no!

Perlooooom! Into the dead centre of the trampoline. Then the strong men pull, harder than ever, and all the crowd has gathered to see and they shriek whooooo! -- as the dogs shoot up up up, smaller and smaller, turning and twirling, seeing the sky, the far fields, the people, the trampoline tinier than a postage stamp.

'Flap flap your paws!' shouts Shaggy. And they flap and they flap and they flap flap flap flap flap – and they're flying.

Out over the fair, over the houses and gardens. 'Bye, bye!' they wave to the people, and they're flying. It's lovely! They're flying along and it's lovely.

And they can see Watkins' farm. They call to the dogs down there and they hear the barks. But they fly on, flap flap flap and it's lovely over the fields.

There's the road, the cars. There's the airfield. They fly on over the woods. It's lovely, lovely, lovely! A crow flies under them and looks back. 'Aaark!' he cries, and nearly falls out of the sky to see two dogs flying.

'Let's glide,' calls Shaggy.
So they stretch their front legs out quite still.
But their paws have no feathers and the two
dogs drop like stones.
'Flap!' howls Shaggy. 'Flap, flap, flap!'

And they flap. They flap. Harder harder harder they flap, as the ground rushes towards them. And they manage, they manage . . .

And they're flying again. Phew! They're flying again and it's lovely, along over the hedges. And the pheasants look up, the hares look up, and a farmer falls off his tractor.

'Here's home,' calls Shaggy. 'Look!'
And their master is in his orchard with his
shotgun shooting at the jackdaws that are
tearing his thatch roof to pieces.
He sees two specks in the sky and swings
his gun and takes aim –

And what does he see?
Not black birds at all.
Shaggy and Spotty come flapping in over the trees.
The farmer drops his gun. They land at his feet.

They jump around barking, barking 'We flew, we flew, we flew all the way!'

But he doesn't know what to make of their barks.
So he gives them each a big bone.

First published in 1997 by Faber and Faber Limited
3 Queen Square London WC1N 3AU

Printed in Belgium by Proost N.V. Turnhourt.

A CIP record for this book
is available from the British Library

ISBN 0–571–19087–1

2 4 6 8 10 9 7 5 3 1